THE
Naughty Crow

· IRINA HALE ·

MARGARET K. McELDERRY BOOKS
New York

Maxwell Macmillan International
New York   Oxford   Singapore   Sydney

Grandfather rocked in his hammock
and watched a distant flight of crows.
"Those birds remind me of
a story..." he said.

First United States Edition 1992

Margaret K. McElderry Books
Macmillan Publishing Company 866 Third Avenue, New York, NY 10022
Macmillan Publishing Company is part of the Maxwell Communication Group of Companies.

Copyright © 1992 by Irina Hale
First published 1992 by William Heinemann Ltd., London, England
The text of this book is set in Sabon.
The illustrations are rendered in ink and watercolor.
Printed in Hong Kong   10 9 8 7 6 5 4 3 2 1

Library of Congress Cataloging-in-Publication Data
Hale, Irina.
The naughty crow / Irina Hale. – 1st U.S. ed.   p.   cm.
"First published 1992 by William Heinemann Ltd., London, England" – T.p. verso.
Summary: The adventures and misadventures of a tame pet crow, owned by a family living in Czarist Russia.
ISBN 0-689-50546-9
[1. Crows – Fiction.   2. Ukraine – Fiction.]   1. Title.
PZ7.H1338Nau   1992   [E] – dc20   91-39929

Once upon a time there were two children,
a boy called Constantine and a girl called Marina.

They lived with their mother and father and their nurse, Niania, in faraway Kiev.

The winter had been long and cold and the children waited impatiently for the snow to melt so that they could leave the town for their house in the country.

Niania packed their toys and clothes, and when everything was ready, the family boarded the paddle steamer that would take them downriver.

It was a long journey, but finally they arrived.
Ivashka, the stable boy, was waiting on the dock,
ready to drive them home.

They climbed into the carriage and rattled along
dusty paths past fields of sunflowers.

Turning into the gates of their summer home,
they saw Avdotia, the cook, Grisha, the gardener,
and Masha, the maid, running to greet them.

The children allowed them-
selves to be hugged and then
went straight up to their room
in the attic to see if everything
was still the same as last year.

Peering out of the window,
they saw something small and
black lying under the tall tree
in the garden.

"What's that?" said Constantine.

"Let's go and see," said Marina.

Down on the grass,
they found a young
crow with an injured
leg. It looked as if it
had tumbled out of
its nest.

"Poor thing," said Marina.

"Let's keep him," said Constantine.
"What shall we call him?"

"Cra-cra," croaked the crow.

So Cra-cra he became.

The children picked up the crow and carried him
carefully into the house to show Niania. She could
cure anything from a pimple to a bad temper.

Niania bandaged the little crow's leg between
two bits of wood to keep it straight.

Immediately, Constantine wanted
a wooden splint for his leg,
and so did Marina.

Cra-cra became very attached to the children. He followed them about all day long and joined in all their games.

He loved bathtime, and as he watched Niania stir handfuls of birch leaves into the water, he would squawk as if to say he wanted to get into the bath too.

It was great fun to have Cra-cra as a pet. But he was a very naughty crow, as the children soon discovered.

One day, they were having an arithmetic lesson
with their tutor when Cra-cra flew into the room.

   He perched on Marina's desk and spilled ink all
over her notebook. Quickly, she shooed him
into the garden.

There, Masha was hanging out the washing. Up
flew Cra-cra, and as fast as Masha hung up the clothes,
Cra-cra picked off the clothespins so that everything
fell down into the mud.

   "That crow must be put in a cage," cried Mamma.
"Immediately."

So when the children were taken to the fair in the village, Cra-cra was left at home. But somehow he managed to peck his way out of his cage and off he flew.

"Look there," said Constantine suddenly. "It's Cra-cra."

The musicians were furious to find
that Cra-cra had pecked a hole in
their drum and Misha the performing
bear looked cross because, in all
the commotion, no one wanted
to watch him dance. Marina and
Constantine were hurried home.
Cra-cra was in disgrace.

The children decided to play dressing up in
Mamma's bedroom instead.

"I'm St. George," said Constantine, brandishing a
broom and sitting on the back of Buria, their dog.

"I'm the princess," said Marina. "What shall we
do for a dragon?"

"Cra-cra can be the dragon," declared Constantine.

Cra-cra didn't want to be a dragon. With a
squawk, he flew out of reach, frightening Buria,
who threw Constantine to the floor. Mamma's powder
was spilled and her necklace dropped onto the carpet.
Cra-cra swooped down for it and then flew straight
out of the window.

Cra-cra took refuge in the tall tree, the necklace
still in his beak.

Marina ran into the garden after him.

"Come down immediately, you naughty bird,"
she shouted. She started to climb up the tree, but
her petticoat caught on a branch and she was stuck.

Everyone came running. Cra-cra was frightened
and dropped the necklace and Marina had to be
rescued with a ladder. Cra-cra was in disgrace again.

Then came Marina's birthday. A picnic was planned and the cousins invited. Constantine had to stay at home to make sure that Cra-cra behaved himself.

"It's not fair," complained Constantine.

"Cra!" said the crow.

"I hope it rains on their horrid picnic."

"Cra-cra!" said the crow.

"I hope a carriage wheel falls off," said Constantine.

"Cra-craah!" said the crow with a naughty gleam in his eye.

Before long the family returned, wet through and on foot.

"You'll never guess what happened," said Marina. "It poured with rain, our carriage got stuck in the mud, and a wheel came off. We were all so cross."

"And for once we couldn't blame your crow," joked Papa. "Has he been good?"

"Very good!" said Constantine.

He spoke too soon. When they all filed into the dining room for the birthday feast they discovered Cra-cra and his friends had flown in through the window.

They wanted to come to the party.

"This is too much," thundered Papa. "That bird
has got to go."

   Oh, how the children cried. But the parents were
firm. No more Cra-cra.

The next day the children had to put Cra-cra in a basket, and Ivashka drove them a long long way to a distant forest where Cra-cra was to be set free.

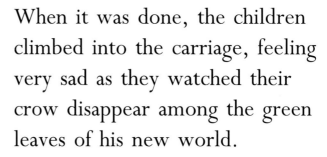

When it was done, the children climbed into the carriage, feeling very sad as they watched their crow disappear among the green leaves of his new world.

"How will he manage without us?" said Marina anxiously.

They clopped back along the forest path until Ivashka stopped to chat with some peasants harvesting wheat.

Suddenly a flight of crows rose in the sky, then swooped toward the trees.

"Look!" Constantine cried out in alarm. "Perhaps they'll hurt Cra-cra."

The children ran back into the forest, but there was no sign of Cra-cra. All around them tall dark trees rose up and the branches creaked and swayed.

"Ivashka! Ivashka!" they cried, but their voices were carried away on the wind.

Then, through the bushes, came a smashing crackling noise louder than any wind. The children huddled together and watched, terrified, as a snout thrust through the bushes.

It was a *bear* ...

… a bear on a chain. Misha, out with his keeper!

"What are you doing, little pigeons, here in the middle of the forest?" asked the keeper.

"We've lost our crow! And our way home," said Marina.

The keeper held up a shiny black feather.

"I found this on the path," he said, pointing behind him.

So they followed the twisting path through the trees until at last they came to the edge of the forest.

There in the distance was their house.

But what was that perching on the veranda?

Could it be? It *was!*–Cra-cra!

He'd flown on ahead and was waiting for them.

The whole household came running down
the steps.

"We were so worried," they cried.

"When Ivashka arrived back without you,
we thought you'd been eaten by wolves."

The keeper introduced himself and
explained how he'd found the children
wandering in the forest.

"It was really Cra-cra who showed us the way home," whispered Marina. "He left us a sign —one of his feathers. Please, please, forgive him and let him stay with us."

Mamma looked at Papa, and Papa nodded his head.

"We'll give him one more chance," he said.

They all sat down to tea and the children told their
adventure all over again.

Suddenly, Papa put his hand to his face.

"That's funny," he said. "I could have sworn I was wearing my spectacles. Where can they be? Cra-cra? CRA-CRA...!"

Grandfather had finished his tale.
"And every bit is true," he said.
"I should know, because that
little boy, Constantine, was me,
once upon a time."